ANNIE AND CLARABEL

Based on *The Railway Series* by the Rev. W. Awdry

Illustrations by
Robin Davies and Creative Design

EGMONT

EGMONT

We bring stories to life

First published in Great Britain 2006
by Egmont UK Limited
239 Kensington High Street, London W8 6SA
Adapted from *Thomas and the Guard* by the Rev. W. Awdry
and *The Runaway* by Christopher Awdry.

Thomas the Tank Engine & Friends™

A BRITT ALLCROFT COMPANY PRODUCTION

Based on The Railway Series by The Reverend W Awdry
© 2006 Gullane (Thomas) LLC. A HIT Entertainment Company

Thomas the Tank Engine & Friends and Thomas & Friends are trademarks of Gullane Entertainment Inc.
Thomas the Tank Engine & Friends is Reg. U.S. Pat. & Tm. Off.

ISBN 978 1 4052 2367 6
ISBN 1 4052 2367 7
1 3 5 7 9 10 8 6 4 2
Printed in Great Britain

*T*his a story about Thomas' coaches, Annie and Clarabel. They love running backwards and forwards along the branch line with Thomas. But one day, they are given a chance to prove just how useful they can really be …

Annie and Clarabel were Thomas' coaches. Annie could only take passengers, but Clarabel could take passengers, luggage and the Guard.

The coaches were old and in need of new paint, but Thomas loved them very much, and they loved him too.

Thomas never got cross with Annie and Clarabel, but he did get cross with other engines on the Main Line who made them late.

One day, Thomas, Annie and Clarabel were waiting for Henry's train to arrive. Henry was late and Thomas was getting crosser and crosser.

"How can I run my train properly if Henry is always late? He doesn't realise that The Fat Controller depends on me," he said.

"I'm sure he'll be along soon," replied Annie and Clarabel, looking around for Henry.

At last, Henry's train arrived.

Thomas was very cross with Henry. But Annie and Clarabel waited patiently as lots of passengers got out of Henry's train, and climbed into them.

Finally, the Guard blew his whistle, and Thomas started at once. But as the Guard turned to jump into Clarabel's van, he tripped over an old lady's umbrella! By the time he had picked himself up, Thomas, Annie and Clarabel were steaming out of the station!

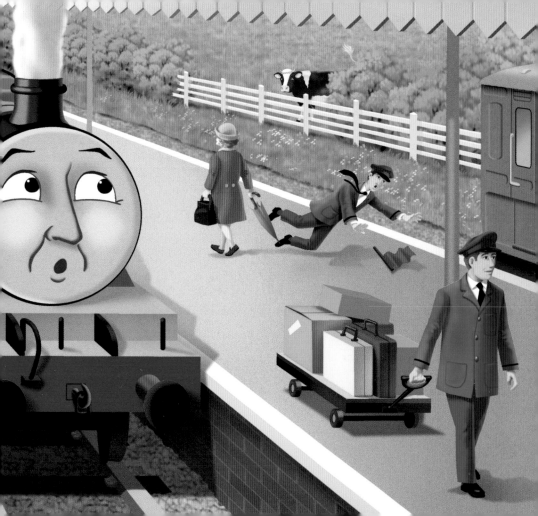

The Guard waved his red flag to stop them, but Thomas and his Driver didn't see him.

"Come along! Come along!" sang Thomas.

"I've lost my nice Guard," sobbed Clarabel.

Annie tried to tell Thomas, "We've left the Guard on the platform!"

But Thomas was too busy hurrying to listen. "Oh, come along!" he puffed impatiently.

Annie and Clarabel tried to pull Thomas back, but Thomas took no notice.

Thomas didn't stop till they came to a signal.

"That silly signal! What's the matter?" Thomas asked his Driver.

"I don't know," replied the Driver. " The Guard will tell us in a minute."

They waited and waited, but the Guard didn't come.

"Peep, peep! Peep, peep! Where is the Guard?" whistled Thomas.

"We tried to tell you ... we've left him behind," sobbed Annie and Clarabel.

Thomas looked back along the line, and there was the Guard, running as fast as he could. Everybody cheered, especially Annie and Clarabel.

"I'm very sorry," said Thomas, when the Guard reached them.

"It wasn't your fault, Thomas. It was the old lady's umbrella," said the Guard, catching his breath. "The signal is down. Let's make up for lost time."

Thomas set off straight away. And Annie and Clarabel sang, "As fast as you like, as fast as you like!" all the way to the end of the line.

A few days later, Thomas was ill and the Big Station couldn't make him better. He would have to go to the Works. Annie and Clarabel were sad. They would really miss Thomas.

Duck came to the station to help while Thomas was away. He was very gentle with Annie and Clarabel and they liked Duck very much.

"He is so calm with such nice manners," they told each other. "It really is a pleasure to go out with him."

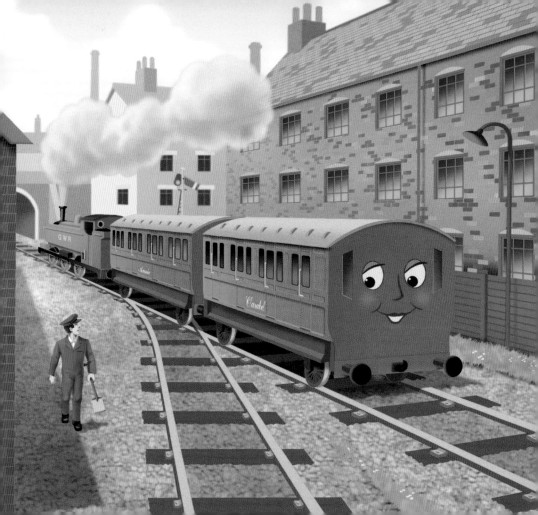

Annie and Clarabel were sorry to say goodbye to Duck when Thomas came home. But they were very pleased to have their old friend back. They told Thomas how well Duck had managed. Thomas was a bit jealous, but he was so pleased to be home that he soon forgot.

The Works had made Thomas feel much better, but they had left his hand brake very stiff. This made his brakes seem as if they were on when they weren't. Thomas' Driver and Fireman soon learnt to be extra careful so they didn't over-run the platform.

But one day, Thomas' Fireman was ill, and a relief Fireman took his place.

Thomas, Annie and Clarabel were waiting for Henry's train to arrive. The Fireman fastened the coupling, but he forgot all about Thomas' hand brake.

Suddenly, Thomas felt his wheels begin to move! He tried to stop, but his Driver and Fireman were on the platform. Thomas, Annie and Clarabel gathered speed out of the station.

"Stop! Stop!" shrieked Annie and Clarabel, but Thomas kept on going.

The Signalman sent a message along the line, and an Inspector prepared to stop Thomas near the airfield. But Thomas was going much too fast for the Inspector to act.

Quickly, the Inspector climbed aboard Harold and they took off.

Below, Thomas was tiring.

"I need to stop, I need to stop," he panted wearily.

Annie and Clarabel knew that they must do something to help their friend.

The coaches remembered how calm Duck was when they worked with him. They must be just as calm and steady now. Annie and Clarabel pulled back as they went uphill and managed to slow poor Thomas down.

As they neared the next station, they saw Harold land and the Inspector run towards the platform. This time, Thomas entered the station slowly enough for the Inspector to jump into his cab, and put the hand brake on hard.

Everyone breathed a sigh of relief as the train stopped.

That evening, The Fat Controller came to see Thomas, Annie and Clarabel.

He told Thomas that he would have his hand brake repaired straight away, and congratulated Annie and Clarabel for helping Thomas when he really needed them.

Annie and Clarabel were delighted, and Thomas beamed with pride. He always knew that they were the best coaches in The Fat Controller's Railway!

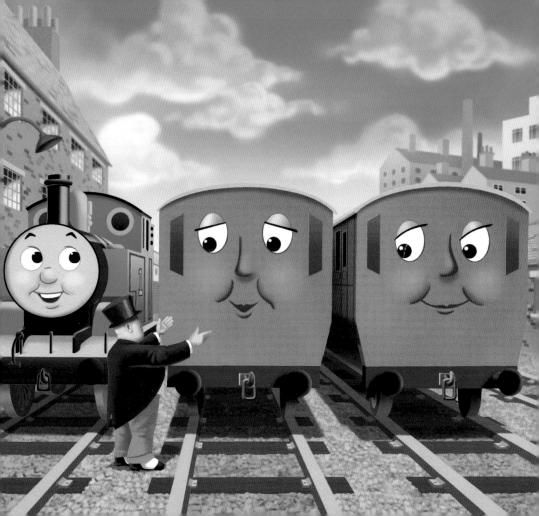

The Thomas Story Library is THE definitive collection of stories about Thomas and ALL his Friends.

5 more Thomas Story Library titles will be chuffing into your local bookshop in Summer 2006:

Fergus
Mighty Mac
Harvey
Rusty
Molly

And there are even more
Thomas Story Library books to follow later!
So go on, start your Thomas Story Library NOW!

A Fantastic Offer for Thomas the Tank Engine Fans!

In every Thomas Story Library book like this one, you will find a special token. Collect 6 Thomas tokens and we will send you a brilliant Thomas poster, and a double-sided bedroom door hanger!
Simply tape a £1 coin in the space above, and fill out the form overleaf.

TO BE COMPLETED BY AN ADULT

To apply for this great offer, ask an adult to complete the coupon below
and send it with a pound coin and 6 tokens, to:
THOMAS OFFERS, PO BOX 715, HORSHAM RH12 5WG

☐ Please send a Thomas poster and door hanger. I enclose 6 tokens
plus a £1 coin. (Price includes P&P)

Fan's name...

Address...

....Postcode...................................

Date of birth...

Name of parent/guardian..

Signature of parent/guardian..

Please allow 28 days for delivery. Offer is only available while stocks last. We reserve the right to change
the terms of this offer at any time and we offer a 14 day money back guarantee. This does not affect your
statutory rights.

☐ Data Protection Act: If you do not wish to receive other similar offers from us or companies we
recommend, please tick this box. Offers apply to UK only.

Cut along the dotted line